TIMOTHY

and the STRONG PAJAMAS

This is the story of ~~WITHDRAWN~~ **TIMOTHY SMALLBEAST.**

He wasn't big.
And he wasn't strong.

(But he really,
really wished he was.)

A superhero adventure by
Viviane Schwarz

ARTHUR A. LEVINE BOOKS
AN IMPRINT OF SCHOLASTIC INC.

This is Timothy!

This is his best friend,
Monkey!

And these are his
favorite pajamas!

Every evening, before he goes to bed,
Timothy tries to make himself stronger.

He drinks a big mug of **fortified milk** and crunches up three **extra-tough cookies.**

He does some exercises.

Then he thinks **STRONG** thoughts.

Doing all that exercise is tough on your pajamas.

"Timothy," said his mother one evening,
"these pajamas are a disgrace.
We must buy you some new ones."

"But these are my favorite pajamas,"
said Timothy. "And they don't sell favorite pajamas
in the stores, they only sell new ones.
Can't you fix them for me? Please?"

So Timothy's mother fixed them for him.

She used the **strongest thread**,

and sewed them **three** times over and **crosswise** to be sure.

She sewed on lots of **sturdy patches**.

She sewed on **six** very red **buttons**,

and an extra **secret** button on the inside.

Timothy was very pleased. "Thank you!" he said. Then he picked Monkey up, and trotted upstairs to bed.

Timothy's mother
had fixed his pajamas so well
that they were now

~ Super Strong Pajamas. ~

Timothy tried his strength out **very carefully.**

He was really,
extremely,
mightily,
amazingly
STRONG.

The next morning, Timothy asked his mother
if he could wear his pajamas all day.
Because it was the weekend,
she said he could.

"Now finish your breakfast,
so you grow up
big and strong!"

Timothy was just wondering how to become a hero when he heard a cry:

Somebody help

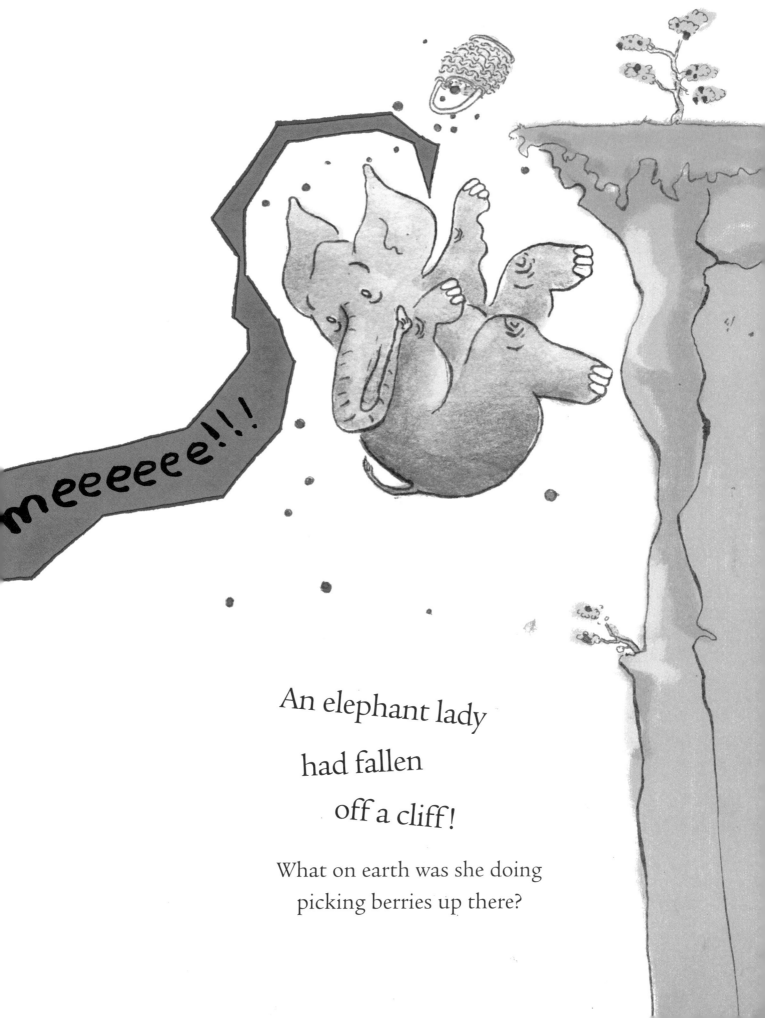

An elephant lady
had fallen
off a cliff!

What on earth was she doing
picking berries up there?

He helped . . .

an old lady . . .

a princess . . .

some sailors . . .

a zookeeper . . .

and a kitten.

At last it was
time to go home.

They were almost home
when they found a **tired bear** crying in the street.
"I can't find the forest," said the bear. "I need to go to sleep for the
winter, but I've lost my way, and now I'm too tired to walk."
"Don't cry," said Timothy. "I'll carry you home."

Now it really was time to go home. "Come on, Monkey," said Timothy.

But Monkey had gone!

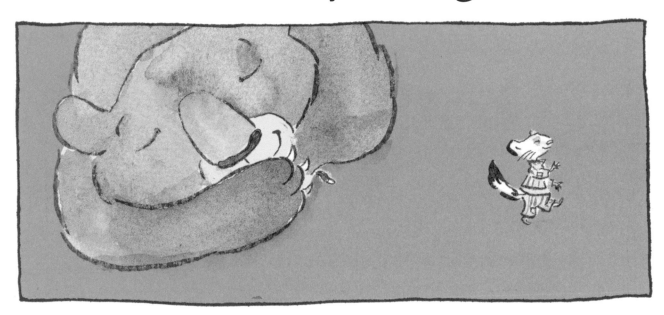

Oh no, he hadn't! He was stuck underneath the bear!
"Don't worry!" said Timothy. "The bear may be fast asleep, but I'll lift him up with my **super strength**, and pull you out."

But when Timothy tried to pull Monkey out,
his pajamas caught on one of the bear's claws, and with a great . . .

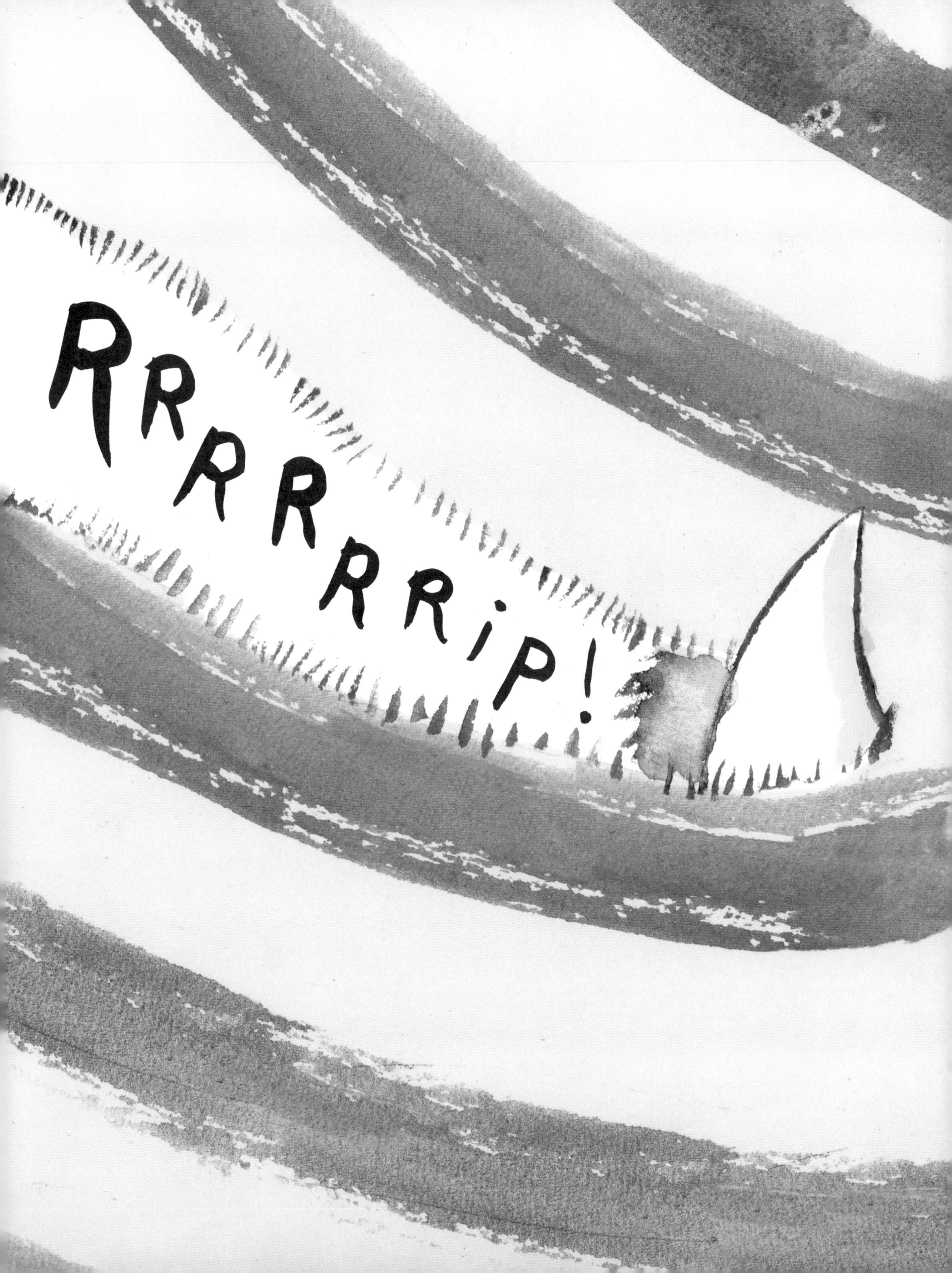
RRRRRRRRip!

His pajamas were not **super strong** anymore!

They were just an old pair of patchy, raggedy pajamas.

And the bear wouldn't wake up until springtime!

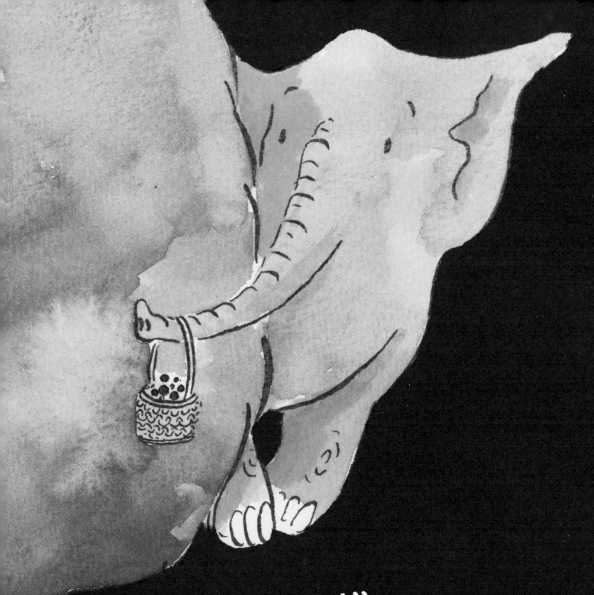

"Oh no!" sobbed Timothy.
"My monkey is being hibernated on by a bear,
and I can't go to sleep without him!
And now I'm not strong anymore because
my pajamas are torn, and I'm only small
and I'm all alone in the forest!"

"That's no good!" said a voice.
It was the Elephant Lady!

She trumpeted a distress signal **so loud** it could be heard for miles and miles around:

COME AND

HELP TIMOTHY!

And here they all came!

Everyone Timothy had helped today:
the old lady, the princess,
the sailors, the zookeeper,
and the kitten.

They all joined together and . . .

"Thank you!" said Timothy.
"Time to go home," said the Elephant Lady.
"I'll give you a lift."

Timothy's mother shook her head
when she saw the state of his pajamas.
"What have you been up to?" she said.

And as Timothy
fell fast asleep with Monkey,
his mother fixed his pajamas
better than ever.

ADVENTURE

THE END

To Mami and to Omi — V. S.

All rights reserved. Published by Arthur A. Levine Books, an imprint of Scholastic Inc., *Publishers since 1920*,
by arrangement with Scholastic Children's Books, London, England.
SCHOLASTIC and the LANTERN LOGO are trademarks and/or registered trademarks of Scholastic Inc.

Library of Congress Cataloging-in-Publication Data
Schwarz, Viviane.
Timothy and the strong pajamas / by Viviane Schwarz. — 1st ed.   p. cm.
Summary: After his mother mends his favorite pajamas, Timothy finds that he has super strength and
decides to use it to help others, but when the pajamas rip again, he loses his strength just when he needs it most.
ISBN-13: 978-0-545-03329-9   ISBN-10: 0-545-03329-2
[1. Pajamas—Fiction. 2. Muscle strength—Fiction. 3. Heroes—Fiction.] I. Title.
PZ7.S41145Tim 2008   [E]—dc22   2007006812

10 9 8 7 6 5 4 3 2 1   08 09 10 11 12
First edition, March 2008   Printed in Singapore

The text was set in ITC Legacy Serif. The display type was set in Slappy Inline.

Design by Lillie Mear